SHORT TALES
Fables

The Fox and the Grapes

Adapted by Christopher E. Long
Illustrated by John Cboins

WAYLAND

WAYLAND

First published in 2013 by Wayland

Copyright © 2013 Wayland

Wayland
338 Euston Road
London NW1 3BH

Wayland Australia
Level 17/207 Kent Street
Sydney, NSW 2000

Adapted Text by Christopher E. Long
Illustrations by John Cboins
Colours by John Cboins
Edited by Stephanie Hedlund
Interior Layout by Kristen Fitzner Denton and Alyssa Peacock
Book Design and Packaging by Shannon Eric Denton
Cover Design by Alyssa Peacock

Copyright © 2008 by Abdo Consulting Group

A cataloguing record for this title is available at the British Library.
Dewey number: 398.2'452-dc23

Printed in China

ISBN: 978 0 7502 7758 7

Wayland is a division of Hachette Children's Books, an Hachette UK company.
www.hachette.co.uk

Fox slept in the cool shade.

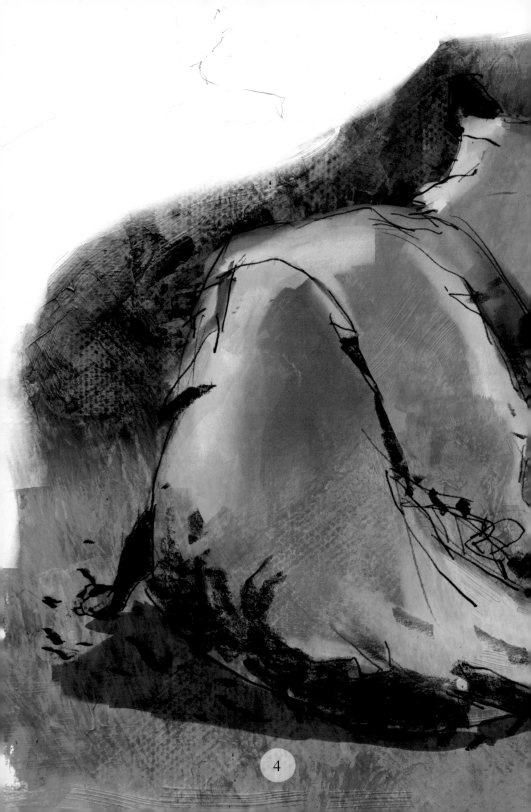

'Fox, you should go and find some lunch' said his mother.

'Someone will bring me something to eat' Fox said.

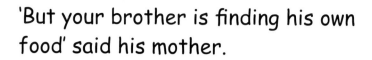

'But your brother is finding his own food' said his mother.

'That apple is too high. Why doesn't he just give up?' Fox asked.

'Because nothing is sweeter than something you have to work to get' his mother said.

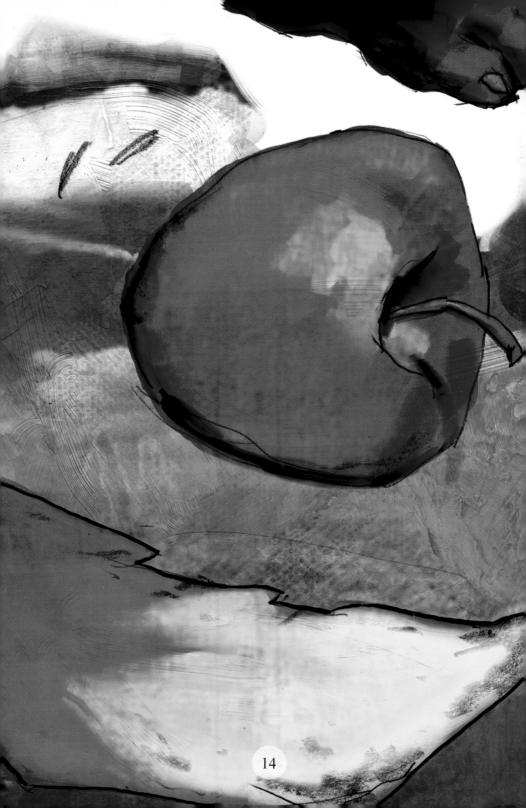

14

Fox did not understand
what his mother meant.

'Brother Fox, have you had lunch?' Fox's brother asked.

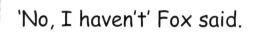

'No, I haven't' Fox said.

'Take my apple' Fox's brother said.

Fox had known someone would bring him something to eat.

Later that day, Fox got hungry.

He walked into the forest to find his family.

'Those grapes look good' Fox said.

Fox jumped high, but he could not reach the grapes.

'I bet those grapes are sour anyway'
Fox said.

The moral of the story is:

It's easy to despise what you cannot have.

SHORT TALES
Fairy Tales

Titles in the Short Tales Fairy Tales series:

Aladdin and the Lamp

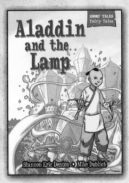

978 0 7502 7750 1

Beauty and the Beast

978 0 7502 7752 5

Jack and the Beanstalk

978 0 7502 7751 8

Puss in Boots

978 0 7502 7754 9

Sleeping Beauty

978 0 7502 7755 6

The Little Mermaid

978 0 7502 7753 2

WAYLAND
www.waylandbooks.co.uk

SHORT TALES
Fables

Titles in the Short Tales Fables series:

The Ants and the Grasshopper

978 0 7502 7756 3

The Boy who cried Wolf

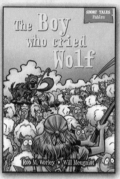

978 0 7502 7757 0

The Fox and the Grapes

978 0 7502 7758 7

The Lion and the Mouse

978 0 7502 7783 9

The Tortoise and the Hare

978 0 7502 7784 6

The Town Mouse and the Country Mouse

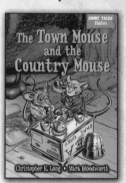

978 0 7502 7785 3

WAYLAND
www.waylandbooks.co.uk

Follow us on Twitter @waylandbooks | Find us on Facebook Wayland Books